Littlenose

More adventures of

Littlenose The Hunter

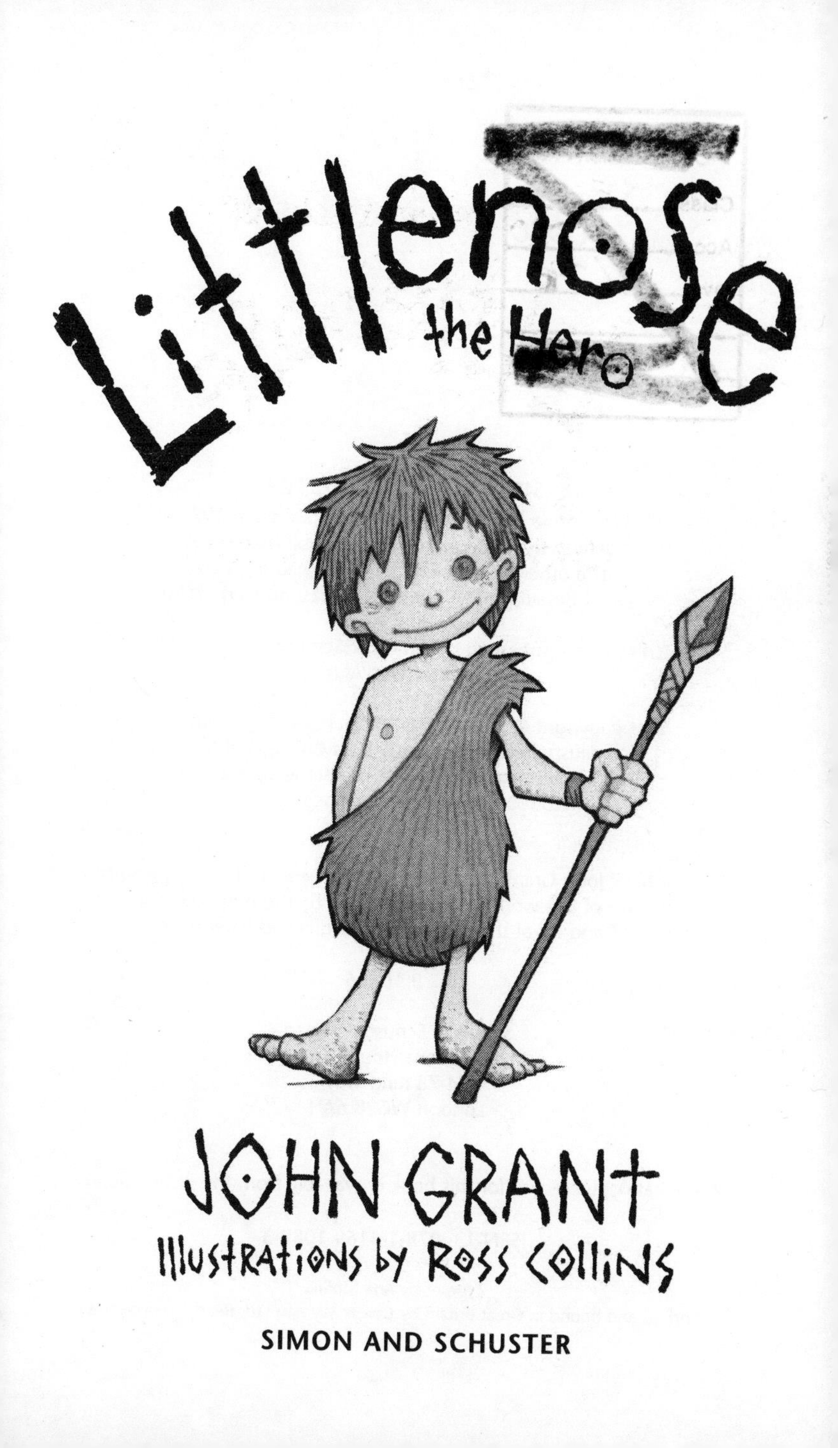

Littlenose the Hero

JOHN GRANT

Illustrations by ROSS COLLINS

SIMON AND SCHUSTER

SIMON AND SCHUSTER
Littlenose the Hero was first published in 1972
Littlenose the Fisherman was first published in 1974
The other stories were first published in 1976
in Great Britain by The British Broadcasting Corporation

This edition published by Simon & Schuster UK Ltd, 2006
A CBS COMPANY

5 7 9 10 8 6

Simon & Schuster UK Ltd
Africa House
64-78 Kingsway
London WC2B 6AH

A CIP catalogue record for this book is available from the British Library

ISBN-13: 978-1-4169-1089-3

Typeset by Ana Molina
Printed and bound in Great Britain by Cox & Wyman Ltd, Reading, Berkshire

Contents

Littlenose Meets Two-Eyes

Littlenose was a boy who lived long, long ago. His people were called the Neanderthal folk. In the days when they lived, the world was very cold. It was called the Ice Age.

There were lots of wild animals. Lions, tigers, bears and wolves had thick furry coats to keep them warm. Even the rhinoceros, and a kind of elephant called a mammoth, were big woolly creatures.

The Neanderthal folk were stocky, sturdy people with short necks and big noses. They were very proud of their noses, which were large and snuffly. Littlenose got his name because his nose was no bigger than a berry.

Littlenose's home was not a house, but a cave where he lived with his mum and dad. Near the front of the cave a huge fire was always burning. This kept the family warm, and also frightened away wild creatures, which was just as well because there was no door on the cave.

Sometimes Littlenose was naughty, and that could be dangerous. A child who strayed from his family cave, or loitered on an errand, might be eaten by a sabre-tooth tiger, or squashed flat as a pancake by a woolly rhinoceros.

But today Littlenose had been very naughty indeed. While his parents were hunting, he had let the fire go out.

Now he sat at the back of the cave and watched Dad trying to relight it. Dad had two stones called flints which he banged together to make a spark. (There were no matches in those days.) But he couldn't strike a spark.

"Perhaps you need a new flint," said Mum.

"I'll need a new son if he lets the fire out again," grumbled Dad. Littlenose expected to be thrown to the bears right away.

However, as they had no fire, Dad blocked the cave entrance with rocks to keep out wild beasts instead.

In the morning they had a cold breakfast. Dad got ready to go for the flint.

"Have you enough money?" said Mum.

"I think so," said Dad, and pulled out a handful of the coloured pebbles which they used for money.

He kissed Mum goodbye, and was just going when Littlenose said, "Can I come too?"

For a moment Dad said nothing. Then: "After the way you behaved, yesterday?" he exclaimed. "Oh, all right," and off he went, leaving Littlenose to follow.

"Goodbye, Littlenose," Mum called after him. "Be good. And always look both ways before you cross."

But Littlenose wasn't listening. He was thinking about his secret. He had a pebble of his own. A green pebble, which he had found by the river. He had never been to a market before. But he was sure he would see something worth buying today.

They made their way by a woodland path. Dad strode along with his club in his hand, and Littlenose skipped gaily behind him. Ahead, the path was crossed by a broad animal trail. Littlenose was about to dash straight across, when a strong arm reached out and grabbed him.

"Don't you *ever* do what your mother tells you?" said Dad, angrily. Shamefaced, Littlenose stood on the grass verge and:

Looked right!

Looked left!

And right again!

As he looked right the second time, a herd of woolly rhinoceros came round the bend. He and Dad dived into the bushes. They lay hidden as the great beasts lumbered by. Their small eyes blinked through their fur, and their long horns looked very dangerous.

When the rhinos had passed, Littlenose and Dad went on their way.

Littlenose felt like he had been walking for ever. But soon they left the woods and began climbing a grassy hillside.

At last they came to a circle of trees. Littlenose realised that this was the market.

There seemed to be hundreds of people. Littlenose hadn't thought there were so many people in the whole world. He trotted behind Dad, and he was bumped, pushed, trodden on, tripped over and shouted at. The sheer noise made him speechless –

but not for long.

Suddenly: "I'm hungry," he said.

"You're always hungry," grumbled Dad. But he bought each of them a steaming hot hunk of meat from a man who was roasting a deer over a fire.

Then he went over to an old man who was sitting under a tree. There was a sign with his name on it.

At least, Littlenose thought it was his name. When he got closer, he saw that it had once read:

SKINS & FLINTS
FOR SALE

But the words had faded with the weather. Only "Skin" and "Flint" could be made out now. Most people thought it was the old man's name.

Neither Dad nor the old man seemed in

a hurry to settle about the new flint. Littlenose soon grew bored.

He wandered through the market, looking here and listening there. Everyone was bustling about buying the things they couldn't find or make for themselves. There were bone and ivory combs, and needles and pins. There were strange nuts, fruits and berries. And there were furs. Hundreds and hundreds of furs. From tiny mink and ermine to enormous white bear skins from the far north.

But Littlenose didn't see anything he wanted to buy. He had almost decided to keep his pebble for another day, when, over the heads of the crowd, he saw a sign:

MAMMOTH SALE
GENUINE REDUCTIONS

Littlenose pushed forward. In a clear space, a little man stood on a tree stump.

"Five red pebbles I'm bid," he shouted. "Five! Going at five! Going! Going! GONE! Sold to the gentleman in the lion-skin for five red pebbles."

The gentleman in the lion-skin counted out his money. Then a huge woolly mammoth was led over to him.

"Oh," thought Littlenose, "if only I could buy one of those. I would march home, leading him by his trunk.

Everyone would cheer. When I got home I would . . . oh dear, no! I forgot. I'm not even allowed pet mice in the cave. Anyway, a mammoth would hardly get its tail through the door. And a tail's about all I could buy with my pebble."

And, feeling very sad, Littlenose walked away. He sat down by the mammoth pen to rest. The pen was built of huge logs and was too high to see over.

Suddenly he jumped. Something soft and warm had tickled his neck.

It was a trunk – a very little one.

Littlenose looked through the bars of the pen.

He saw the smallest, woolliest, saddest mammoth you could imagine. He climbed up and reached over the top rail to stroke its furry ears.

Suddenly he was seized by the scruff of his neck. A voice said, "And what are you doing, young man?"

It was the man who owned the mammoths.

"Please," said Littlenose, "I was just looking at the mammoth."

"Don't tell stories," said the man. "We've sold them all."

But at that moment the trunk came through the bars again. It tickled the man's leg and he dropped Littlenose.

"They've done it again," the man shouted to his assistant, who came running. "Slipped in a reject! It's much too small to sell. And look, the eyes don't match! One's red and one's green. Who's going to buy this sort of animal?"

"I will," said Littlenose, holding out his pebble.

Looking very relieved, the man said, "Well, I can't charge you more than eight white pebbles for a reject." He took the green pebble from Littlenose, and gave him two white ones as change. The assistant opened the pen, and the little mammoth trotted out.

"One red eye and one green eye," said Littlenose. "That makes two eyes. I shall call you that. Come along, Two-Eyes."

Littlenose stopped and bought a bundle of bone needles for Mum with his last two pebbles. The market was almost deserted now.

He started looking for Dad, but Dad found him first.

"Where *have* you been?" he shouted.

"Do you like my mammoth?" asked Littlenose.

"Mammoth? MAMMOTH?" roared Dad. "Are you playing with other people's property? Take it back to where you found it. No, wait, we haven't time." He turned to Two-Eyes, waved his arms in the air, and gave a loud yell. Two-Eyes went scampering into the trees.

"But he's mine. I *bought* him," wailed Littlenose.

But Dad wasn't listening – he was already striding away down the hillside. Littlenose hurried after him. The evening mist began to close in, and the sun became a dull red ball low in the sky.

"Don't dawdle, you'll get lost," called out Dad. But Littlenose kept tripping in the long grass. Each time he looked up it was darker, and even harder to see his father.

He ran on, stumbling and tripping.

Then he fell!

When he got up again, he was alone. "Dad!" he called. "DAD!" But all he heard was the echo of his own voice.

He began to run. He had never been lost before, and he was very frightened. All sorts of terrible things might be waiting in the mist to jump out at him. As he ran, the sun set. It became pitch dark . . .

All around him he could hear animals growling and snorting. They rustled in the undergrowth, and brushed past him as he ran. He stopped to catch his breath. There was a sound behind him. It was growing louder.

Littlenose began to run again. But, as fast as he ran, the noise came closer. Suddenly he tripped again and fell.

Too frightened to move, Littlenose lay with his eyes closed. The sound grew louder. He could hear an animal breathing, but he dared not look up.

At the cave, Mum looked out as darkness fell. There was a sound of footsteps, and Dad groped his way in.

"Where's Littlenose?" asked Mum.

"Isn't he here?" said Dad. "I thought the young rascal must have hurried home ahead of me."

"Oh," said Mum, "he must be lost out there in the dark. You must find him!"

Quickly, Dad lit the fire, took a branch for a torch, and turned back the way he had come.

The mist had gone and the moon was shining. The path lay clear before him.

There were animal sounds among the trees. But there was no sign of Littlenose.

Then something moved towards him. Dad's torch glinted on a pair of eyes. One red eye. One green eye. It was a small mammoth, and sitting on its back was Littlenose.

"Hello, Dad," he said. "I got lost, and Two-Eyes followed me and brought me home."

Mum saw the strange procession approaching the cave. Dad was leading Two-Eyes by the trunk. Littlenose, his head nodding, sat on the mammoth's back.

A few moments later, Mum was tucking Littlenose into bed. He held out a little bundle.

"I bought you some needles at the market," he said, and fell asleep.

The little mammoth was waiting patiently outside. Dad took its trunk gently in his hand. He led it past the fire and into the corner where Littlenose slept. With a contented sigh and looking for all the world like an enormous ball of wool, Two-Eyes fell asleep as well.

The Sun Dance

The days when Littlenose lived were what we now call the Ice Age because much of the land was hidden under a great mass of ice.

The summers were only *just* warm, and in winter, gales and blizzards swept down from the ice-covered mountains, while the people huddled over roaring fires in their draughty caves and waited for spring.

One cold winter's day when the snow lay thick over everything, and the wind screamed and howled outside the cave, Littlenose was sitting by the fire with his mum and dad.

Mum and Dad were talking together in low voices. "I still think he's too young to be told," said Mum. "He won't understand."

"He's got to know some time," replied Dad, "and now is as good a time as any.

You wouldn't want him to grow up knowing nothing about it, would you now?"

He turned to Littlenose, who had been listening with one ear anyway, and said, "Littlenose, you're getting to be a big boy, and there's something you must know. Listen carefully, and I'll explain."

"I still think he's too young," said Mum, but Dad gave her a look and went on.

"In summer, the sun is warm. It melts the snow, opens the flowers, ripens the fruit and warms the breeze. Now, this is very hard work, and like any hard work, it makes the sun very, very tired. Now, Littlenose, tell me: what happens in autumn when the fruit is ripe?"

"It gets cold," said Littlenose.

"Quite right," said Dad, "and have you ever stopped to think why?"

Littlenose, who rarely stopped to think of anything, said, "No."

"Well," continued Dad, "I'll tell you. All the effort of making things grow leaves the sun very weak indeed. As the year goes on, it gives out less and less heat. It rises late and sets early, and soon has barely enough strength to rise above the horizon. Just now it is so feeble that a heavy shower of rain might wipe it out altogether. If the sun is not to die and leave us without light and warmth, then something has to be done every year to keep it going for another summer. So far, you have been too little to take part, but now you will do your bit . . . starting tomorrow. In three days' time is the Sun Dance."

The next three days were very busy for Littlenose, and indeed for the whole tribe.

First of all they worked hard clearing all the snow from a flat circle of ground among the trees.

Next, they went into the woods and gathered green branches. They found yew and fir, and holly with masses of round, red berries. They cut long streamers of ivy from the rocks and tree trunks. They climbed trees to bring down clusters of bright green mistletoe with white berries, and collected armfuls of white laurel. From the hillsides they cut sprays of green broom and gorse, the last of which Littlenose didn't like one bit, as it scratched his arms and prickled his fingers. All this greenery was piled in the clearing until there was barely room to move.

But they weren't finished yet.

Some of the men went off into the woods

again with their flint axes, and after a great deal of labour reappeared looking tired but pleased with themselves, and dragging a slender spruce tree. They pulled it into the clearing and, after much effort by everyone, and a good deal of shouting and confusion, it was set upright in the ground.

Now everyone began to help decorate the clearing with the tree branches.

The ivy was strung between the tree trunks, with clusters of holly and mistletoe at intervals along it.

More holly and mistletoe were entwined with the fir, laurel, gorse and broom to form wreaths and garlands and sprays. These were fixed on the bare trunks and branches of the trees until, compared with the bare snow-covered land around it, the clearing began to look like a little bit of summer that had been left over.

"This," explained Dad, "is what we are trying to do. We will show the sun what summer is like, so that it will remember, and we shall light fires to warm it and give it back some of its strength. There will also be, of course, singing and feasting and dancing. And we'll all get presents."

"This," thought Littlenose, "gets better every minute."

The day of the Sun Dance came at last. Littlenose was out early, and anxiously watched the sun as it rose above the hills. It seemed to be hardly moving, but at last the dull red ball was in full view. It didn't look at all healthy, and Littlenose hoped that they weren't going to be too late.

At last, dressed in his best furs, Littlenose set off with his parents.

The clearing was crowded. Everyone was happy and smiling, but nothing appeared to be happening yet. Then everyone fell silent and looked towards the spruce tree, which was decorated with holly berries, and hung with intriguing bundles. The Old Man was standing by the tree with a lit torch in his hand, and Littlenose saw that a huge unlit fire had been prepared. The topmost log of the fire was decorated like the trees.

Facing the sun, which was slipping below the horizon, the Old Man began to sing, while the people clapped their hands in time with him. Then everyone gradually joined in, till the sound of singing and clapping shook the snow from the trees.

Suddenly, the singing and clapping stopped. The Old Man stepped forward, held his torch towards the sun and said something in a loud voice. He said it again, and Littlenose somehow expected the sun to jump back up into the darkening sky.

But it didn't.

The Old Man thrust his torch into the fire, which burst into flames. At the same time, smaller fires around the edge of the clearing were lit. Food was brought out in quantities which made Littlenose's eyes pop with wonder.

First, there was fruit. Crab apples and pears, brown-skinned and wrinkled but soft and sweet inside. There were sticky red berries from the dark woods and hips, haws and brambles from the thickets by the river. There were all manner of nuts. Chestnuts, beechnuts, hazels, walnuts, acorns and even earth-nuts.

Then, from the river, were trout, salmon, crayfish and mussels.

Littlenose could hardly enjoy one thing for hurrying on to the next. He stuffed his mouth full, and for once no one told him to mind his manners.

All this time, a crowd of women had been busy around the big fire. A delicious smell began to drift across the clearing.

Littlenose, thinking the wonders would never end, went to investigate.

A giant ox was being roasted over the flames. Gravy dripped and sizzled, and the smell nearly drove Littlenose mad with impatience. The meat was almost ready, and in a few minutes Littlenose was wolfing down his share with gusto. Served with the roast ox were also mushrooms, truffles and all kinds of sweet-tasting roots and bulbs.

Littlenose was beginning to think that perhaps even he couldn't eat another mouthful, when pieces of honeycomb were passed round. The wax was crisp and the honey had turned partly to sugar. Littlenose crunched and munched, and thought that he was the happiest boy in the whole world.

The food was cleared away, and the singing

and dancing began. Everyone clapped the dancers who leapt and whirled, pretending to be birds, animals, hunters and even fish. Everyone joined in the singing, and Littlenose, who didn't know all the songs,

joined in just the same . . .

When Littlenose was almost nodding with tiredness, the Old Man stood up and everyone became quiet.

He stood by the decorated spruce tree and the tribe waited eagerly. Then, one by one, he called their names. As each person went forward they were given one of the little bundles from the tree.

Mum's contained a bone comb. Dad got a new barbed point for his fishing spear. And Littlenose? He was speechless with delight. He was given two small flints! He felt really grown-up. He could light his own fires now . . .

And that was almost the end of another Sun Dance.

Just before they returned to their caves, the people all stood, while the Old Man stretched out his arms and cried, "We have had warmth and light and laughter. May the Great Sun grow in strength from day to day and bring us yet another summer."

And, do you know . . . It did!

The Painted Cave

In the days when Littlenose lived, men painted pictures on the walls of caves. In some parts of the world, you can still see the pictures they made. They show mammoths, deer, horses and rhinoceros, as well as men hunting and women dancing.

However, it was not Littlenose's people, the Neanderthal folk, who painted the caves. They might occasionally scratch a rough outline of a lion or a hyena on a bone or piece of stone, and Littlenose sometimes made pictures in the wet sand or in the dust, but the secret of mixing colours and making lifelike drawings of animals belonged to the Straightnoses.

Now, the Straightnoses were great hunters, and part of their success in hunting lay in *magic*!

And this was why they painted the caves. These caves were very special and secret places, only visited by the hunters and leaders of the Straightnose tribes. If they were planning a deer hunt, say, they would come to the cave and perform magical dances and sing spells and enchantments before a picture of a deer, and this ensured that the hunt would be successful.

Littlenose, of course, knew nothing of all of this.

One day, he and Two-Eyes, with Mum and Dad, were far from home. Dad had heard of a place where flints could be dug out of the ground, which was cheaper than buying them; and so, armed with a pick fashioned from a deer's antler, they had set off before daylight. Now Dad was banging and hacking away at the chalky hillside in a great cloud of white dust, and had already unearthed some first-class flints.

Two-Eyes, as usual, had gone to sleep, while Mum was preparing a picnic lunch.

Littlenose had discovered a small stream, and was playing one of his favourite games: dropping twigs into the water and watching them sail along until they were out of sight. After a while, he thought it would be fun to follow the twigs and see where they went.

The stream had cut itself a deep channel, and, after a short distance, the grass and bushes grew right over to form a green tunnel.

Littlenose ran after the twigs, and under the green

arch. It was rather exciting, and he hurried splashing along. Suddenly, he noticed that it had become darker. He looked up. The sides of the tunnel were still earth and rock but so was the roof. He looked back. He had been so busy watching his twigs that he hadn't noticed that the stream had left the open, and was flowing into a dark hole in the ground.

Forgetting all his father's warnings about going into strange caves, Littlenose decided to explore. He splashed into the tunnel, which was just high enough for him to stand upright. It was fairly straight, and enough light came in for him to see by. He kept glancing behind him, and decided he would turn back when he could no longer see the entrance. On he went. It was chilly and dark and he disturbed several bats which went fluttering and twittering past his head.

Then the tunnel turned sharp right. Littlenose hesitated, looked back at the light for a moment, and carried on.

Immediately, he could see light ahead of him.

"It must be the end," thought Littlenose.

But it wasn't sunlight. It was flickering and yellow, and also the stream was beginning to run faster and to make a loud splashing sound up ahead. Littlenose splashed the last few metres . . . and stopped in amazement.

The tunnel did not end in daylight.

It stopped high up in the side of a huge cavern, while the stream splashed its way down the rock face and into a dark pool at the foot. The cavern was lit by a number of torches made of pine branches stuck into cracks in the rock. But, most remarkable of all, the walls were covered with pictures.

Now occasionally, Littlenose did very silly things, and he ought to have known that a cave that had pictures *and* torches burning must belong to *someone*; but, without hesitation, he scrambled down the rocks and ran to have a closer look.

He had never seen anything like it before. There were pictures of mammoth herds, galloping horses, charging bulls, and a whole party of hunters with spears.

There was one particular picture of a huge bison which looked very new.

In fact, the paint still looked wet . . . and Littlenose patted it with his hand to make sure. It *was* wet, and Littlenose got paint all over the palm of his hand, but he cleaned it off on the rock, leaving red hand-prints, then wiped his hand on his furs.

He was still admiring the pictures when he heard the oddest sound. He turned, and cocked his head to listen. He just couldn't work out what it was, but it was rather frightening, and it was getting louder. He stood still until he realised that it was voices he was hearing. Men's voices, echoing among the rocks!

Littlenose scrambled for dear life up the rocks to his tunnel, and watched.

The noise was almost deafening when, from an opening at the opposite side of the cave, a long line of men came marching. At least, Littlenose *thought* they were men. They walked upright, but their bodies were covered with strange-coloured patterns. Some of them even appeared to have animals' heads! But it was the leader who was the most ferocious. He was the most hideously painted, and his head was hidden under a great mass of shaggy hair from which protruded two sharp bison horns. In each hand he carried a long, red-pointed spear.

The procession halted in front of the newly-painted bison. Some men squatted in a semi-circle with short sticks in their hands. The rest stood behind, while the leader stood facing them with his arms outstretched.

The men started clapping their hands and beating their sticks together, and the leader tossed his bison horns and began to dance, while singing in a high-pitched voice. More men joined in the dance, which became fast and furious, while all joined in the singing which rang and echoed around the cave.

Faster grew the dancing, and louder the singing. They whirled, spun and leapt, the flickering torches casting a weird light and making the painted animals seem almost alive. Littlenose leaned forward in excitement.

The dancers had fallen back, now, and the leader was alone in front of the bison. The singing stopped as he raised his spears.

Littlenose leaned further forward.

His hand touched a loose rock.

With a resounding splash, it toppled into the pool.

Instantly, the crowd turned. The leader pointed up at Littlenose and screamed.

Littlenose fled!

Back along the tunnel he splashed and stumbled.

Shouting and screaming, his pursuers scrambled up the rocks. They were so anxious to catch him that they climbed over each other, and in their haste some missed their footing and fell head first into the pool.

Littlenose looked back as he ran. He was leaving his pursuers behind. He could run upright, but they had to bend low, and kept banging their heads on the rocky roof and stumbling in the stream.

He reached the corner and looked back again.

The Straightnoses had given up, and had gone back to their interrupted dance.

Littlenose hurried to where the daylight shone through the overhanging leaves, and out into the open air. He sat down on the grass for a moment to get his breath back, then set off to rejoin his parents . . . wondering what on earth Mum would say when she saw the red paint on his good furs.

After the Straightnoses had finished their magic dance, you might think that they would be very annoyed at the mess Littlenose had made with the paint, and would clean his hand-marks off the wall. But if you look carefully in the caves in Lascaux, in France, you can see not only lots of beautifully painted animals, but also a number of hand-prints.

Could they be Littlenose's, do you think?

Littlenose the Musician

The tribe to which Littlenose belonged was like a very large family with all the members related to each other, so Littlenose had a great many aunts and uncles. One uncle was Littlenose's particular favourite. He liked his other relatives, and loved his mum and dad very much, but not one of them was as special as Uncle Redhead.

To begin with, he had flaming red hair,

with a beard to match, unlike the other Neanderthals, who were very dark. Then, he could do the most remarkable things. He could light a fire by *rubbing sticks* as well as by striking flints! He could make painted pictures of animals! *And* he could tell stories.

He would sit for hours, recounting strange and sometimes terrifying tales of the barren lands to the north, where the musk oxen roamed, the white bears hunted, and icy rivers flowed from the great Ice Cap. Or perhaps he might describe the sunny land to the south where fish swam in a warm sea, and the fruit was bigger and sweeter than anyone could imagine.

Uncle Redhead was also very generous. He never visited without bringing gifts. It might be new flints for Dad, a beautiful fur from some strange animal for Mum, and for Littlenose? Well, he could never guess, but it was always something strange and exciting.

One morning, Dad sat mending a spear, while Mum was patching a pair of Littlenose's furs. Dad looked very gloomy. Uncle Redhead was back again.

Dad looked at Mum. "After all, he's YOUR brother," he said.

"Step-brother," replied Mum, "and it's not my fault he's so clever."

"That's just the trouble," said Dad. "He's too clever by far. It's not right. If you ask me, there's something odd about him . . . a touch of—" (and here Dad lowered his voice to a whisper) "—a touch of Straightnose!"

"Straightnose!" gasped Mum.

"All these tricks of his," went on Dad. "What other Neanderthal can swim, for instance? Or make fire with sticks? And his wanderings! He doesn't live in a cave. He doesn't belong to a tribe. He's not respectable."

"But he's so kind," said Mum, "and Littlenose adores him."

"Littlenose also adores his mammoth," snorted Dad, "but at least Two-Eyes doesn't put crazy notions into the boy's head."

At that moment Littlenose trotted up with Two-Eyes.

"Where's Uncle Redhead?" he asked.

"He went out hunting early this morning," said Mum. "He's a very good hunter."

"Too good," muttered Dad, darkly.

At that moment, there came a loud shout, and Uncle Redhead strode out of the trees, a haunch of venison on his shoulder.

"Hullo, there," he called. "This is all I could carry. I've hung the rest of the meat on a tree where the foxes can't get it. We can collect it later."

"What a good idea," said Mum. Dad only grunted.

"Uncle Redhead! Uncle Redhead!" shouted Littlenose. "You haven't given me my present yet!"

"Littlenose!" exclaimed Mum, but Uncle Redhead only laughed.

"You're quite right to remind me, lad, but I hadn't forgotten. We're going to fetch it now."

Taking Littlenose by the hand, Uncle Redhead strode away up the river bank. Littlenose had to run to keep pace with his uncle's long stride, but after a little while they turned away from the river, and Uncle Redhead said, "This'll do, I think."

Littlenose looked around, puzzled. "But . . . my present!" he wailed.

"All right, all right," said Uncle Redhead. "In a moment. Just sit here and watch carefully."

Littlenose sat down on a boulder.

Uncle Redhead walked over to a clump of tall hemlock, which waved and nodded its creamy flowerheads in the breeze. Very carefully, he took his flint knife and cut a handful of the stalks. He sat down beside Littlenose and said, "Now, watch."

He took a jointed stem, and cut it short just above a joint; then he slit the stem part way down its length, and handed it to Littlenose.

"Now," he said, "blow!"

Rather puzzled, Littlenose put the end of the stalk in his mouth and blew hard.

He almost dropped it as it gave out a loud droning sound. He blew it again, and again it made the sound. Littlenose was delighted. He blew long notes. He blew short notes. He blew loudly. And he blew very softly.

He stopped for breath, and found that Uncle Redhead had been busy with more stalks. They were each of different thicknesses, and when Littlenose blew them, they all made different notes. He was so excited he couldn't speak. He wanted to go on blowing and blowing. But his uncle took them from him, and carefully bound them side by side with strips of bark. Then Littlenose found he could easily blow them one after the other, or even two together, and make the most wonderful music. He pranced up and down, blowing his pipes with great gusto, so that the birds stopped chirping to listen, and small animals peered from the among the leaves and branches at the marvellous sound.

At last, Littlenose dropped breathlessly on to his rock.

"Uncle Redhead," he gasped, "this is the most wonderful present I've ever had."

"I'm glad you like it," said his uncle, "but come along; it's time we were getting home."

When they arrived at the cave, they found that quite a crowd had gathered. Everyone looked very worried, even frightened, and they all began shouting to Uncle Redhead and Littlenose, "Did *you* hear it? What was it?"

"What was what?" asked Littlenose.

"The noise," they all said. "You must have heard it! It came from up the river. A strange whistling and droning, like wind in the treetops, and bees swarming, and . . ."

"Oh, you mean like this," said Littlenose, and pulling his pipes from under his furs he blew merrily up and down the scale.

Everyone shrank back fearfully. "What is it?" they asked.

"Uncle Redhead made it for me," said Littlenose. "It makes music." And he blew it again.

"Uncle Redhead," muttered Dad, as the crowd dispersed. "I might have known it!"

At lunch, Uncle Redhead announced

that he was leaving that afternoon.

"Got to keep moving along, you know," he said, and while Dad looked very relieved, Littlenose almost cried with disappointment.

The weeks after Uncle Redhead's departure went by, and to everyone's relief Littlenose gradually forgot about his pipes. In any case, Dad had said that he was only to play them where no one could hear, which was difficult, as the piercing notes carried for a very long way indeed.

One warm day when the summer was almost over, Littlenose and Two-Eyes went exploring. They thought there might be some early fruit ripe for eating in the woods farther up the river. They found some brambles and elderberries and ate as many as they could. Then, feeling very sleepy, they lay down in the warm sun in the shelter of a mossy bank. They had been asleep for quite some time when Littlenose woke suddenly to find Two-Eyes standing up, his ears spread wide, and his trunk held out sniffing the breeze.

"What is it, Two-Eyes?" asked Littlenose, but the little mammoth just stood, watching and sniffing. Then, Littlenose's heart almost stopped with fright as he saw a movement among some low bushes, and a huge, striped hyena move slowly out into the sunlight.

Had it seen them? Littlenose decided not to wait to find out. Tugging at Two-Eyes' fur, he started to scramble up the bank . . . and in a moment he'd slid right to the bottom again! Again he tried. And again he slid down. It was so wet and slippery with green moss that he just couldn't keep a grip, while Two-Eyes couldn't even get started.

Littlenose looked around in panic, but there was no other way out. The undergrowth and bushes were thick and thorny, and the only open space was straight ahead, where the hyena now lay with its head in its paws, flicking its ears to drive away the flies, and watching and waiting. Littlenose knew that hyenas were cowardly animals which attacked by creeping up and taking their victims by surprise. He knew that as long as he stayed awake, or as long as it was light, he was safe; but it was already late afternoon and the sun was moving steadily down the sky.

He wondered if they could tiptoe past. But, as soon as they moved away from the bank, the hyena slowly stood up, keeping its eyes firmly fixed on them.

Perhaps he could drive it away. Picking up a stone, Littlenose threw it as hard as he could. But his small arm was not strong enough: the stone fell in the grass, and the hyena hardly glanced at it.

"We'll have to get help, Two-Eyes," said Littlenose. "Now, both together, as loud as you can. One. Two. Three. H-E-L-P!" And Two-Eyes trumpeted and Littlenose shouted, both as hard as they could.

The hyena jumped back at the sound, and the birds flew out of the trees, screeching with fright. In fact, the birds made so much noise that they quite drowned Littlenose's cries. He shouted himself hoarse, but he soon realised that no one was likely to hear him, certainly neither Mum nor Dad back at the cave. If only his voice were strong enough to carry! If only Uncle Redhead were here! He would know what to do.

Uncle Redhead! Of course! Littlenose hardly dared hope. He remembered the day the people had heard the sound of his pipes coming from a distance. He was sure he was no further away today. He put his hand inside his furs, into the secret pocket where he kept his special treasures, and pulled out his pipes. He had forgotten all about them, and now the hemlock stems had dried and withered to a bruised and bent bundle of dead twigs. Even before he tried, Littlenose knew it was hopeless, but nevertheless, he put them to his lips and blew . . . and nothing happened.

Littlenose threw down the useless pipes, and looked at the sun, which was now level with the treetops. The hyena had also noticed this, and was pacing to and fro. Littlenose watched it, and as he did so his eye caught something white waving gently in the wind. He looked closely. Yes, it was a small clump of hemlock, almost hidden by the long grass and overhanging bushes. And it was terribly close to the hyena.

Slowly, Littlenose inched his way forward, while the hyena backed away a step or two, waiting to see what would happen. Reaching the clump, Littlenose broke off the thickest stem he could see, and edged his way back to Two-Eyes, never taking his eyes off the hyena.

He had no knife, but he found a sharp stone and began to cut at the hemlock stem as best he could, trying to remember how Uncle Redhead had done it. The result was pretty ragged, but, taking an enormous breath, Littlenose put it to his lips and blew with all his might.

At home, Mum was preparing supper, and Dad was putting wood on the fire, when suddenly the air was split by a deep booming sound.

"What was that?" said Dad, jumping up and dropping sticks all over the place.

The sound came again.

And again!

"It's Littlenose," exclaimed Mum, "with

that thing which Redhead gave him. I thought he'd forgotten all about it."

"I'll give him 'Redhead'," shouted Dad. "Why, we'll have the neighbours complaining any minute, and they've only just started speaking to us again." And, leaving the fire, he strode off in the direction of the sound.

It was getting dark when Dad at last caught sight of Littlenose, who was still frantically blowing. Dad was about to rush forward and shout at him when he saw a suspicious movement in the long grass. The hyena, feeling bold now in the growing darkness, was creeping up, his mind filled with thoughts of a fine two-course supper of boy and mammoth.

Now, maybe Dad didn't know much about music, but he was an expert at throwing stones. Within seconds the hyena's hungry hopes were dashed by a large rock which bounced off his bony skull. Then stones started to rain down on him as if the very sky were falling. Bruised, winded, and yelping with terror, the hyena fled into the night.

As the hyena's howls died in the distance, Littlenose threw himself into his dad's arms.

They were about to go when Dad bent down and picked up the hemlock stick. "You mustn't forget your pipe," he said. And Littlenose clutched it tightly in his hand as they made their way safely home to Mum.

Littlenose's Voyage

Littlenose loved the river. It flowed past the cave where he lived with Mum and Dad and Two-Eyes. The river flowed smoothly, except when the snow melted in the spring; then its surface was broken by curling waves which reminded Littlenose of the sea. Then, too, the river brought down trees, bushes and even dead animals, and carried them swiftly past and far away.

One hot summer day, Littlenose was stretched out in the long grass watching the river. The sun was shining, insects hummed, and Two-Eyes lazily flapped his ears from time to time to drive them away.

There was a long sandspit which reached out from the bank, ending in a small patch of beach. Littlenose lay above the beach and imagined himself floating along on the river.

He watched a fallen tree caught in a tangle of dead branches, which bobbed gently in the current.

"I wonder where that came from?" he thought. "And will it end up as firewood in somebody's cave? Or will it float all the way to the sea, and be lost for ever?" He turned to Two-Eyes. But Two-Eyes had gone.

Littlenose decided that he too might as

well go home. It seemed a long time since lunch, and he might manage a small snack if Mum were about . . . or a large one if she weren't. He walked along to where the dark woods came down to the river's edge.

And there he met the bear! Luckily, he saw the bear before the bear saw him.

Under the trees were patches of black shadow, and as Littlenose approached, one of the patches suddenly rose up, stretched, and gave an enormous yawn. It was a huge black bear. It had been sleeping in the cool of the woods when Littlenose's footsteps had disturbed it. Now it stood, still half-asleep, peering blearily and wondering what was happening. Littlenose didn't wait for it to find out. He ran away as fast as he could.

After a moment he looked back. The bear was turning its head this way and that, and for a moment Littlenose thought it was going back to sleep. But instead it dropped on all fours and came swiftly towards him.

Littlenose ran even faster this time. Out along the sandspit he fled, with the bear in hot pursuit. Across the beach he went. The river was on three sides of him, with the bear rushing up on the fourth.

He was trapped. No, not quite.

Quickly he splashed into the shallow water, scrambled through the tangled branches of the fallen tree, and climbed on to the trunk. The tree rocked alarmingly as the bear tried to follow Littlenose, but the branches were too close together for it to get at him.

Again and again the bear tried to pull itself up, but the dead branches broke under its weight. Littlenose clung on, leaning as far as possible from the furious animal.

Then the bear made one more effort. It drew back and stood snarling, water streaming from its fur, and eyes ablaze with rage, then threw itself forward with a roar. It lunged madly at the log and seized a branch with both paws. It had pulled itself partly on to the log when the branch gave way, and the bear fell back with a loud splash.

The tree rocked and rolled wildly, but Littlenose hung on grimly and saw the bear swimming back to the shore.

He was safe. Or was he?

The bear was *swimming*!

The tree was no longer aground in shallow water, but had drifted out from the shore. Already the current was beginning to carry it downstream, and Littlenose watched the beach get farther and farther away. He could hardly make out the sandspit now, and couldn't see the bear at all. The last thing he saw before the current carried him round a bend was a trickle of smoke from the cave.

"Oh dear," he thought, "I'm going to be late for supper." But he wasn't very worried. He was sure that the log would soon drift towards the shore.

However, as the afternoon passed, the log kept a steady course down the river. Littlenose no longer had any idea where he was. Thick woods lined either bank, and he could see no signs of life. He began to think of all the rubbish he often watched floating past the cave. He had wondered where it went. Now he was going to find out.

Littlenose looked left and right, and tried

to judge whether the log was drifting towards one shore or the other. Then he noticed he was coming to a line of trees and bushes. "The river must bend," he thought. "I'll soon be ashore!" The log drifted on slowly now, but the gap narrowed all the time.

At last Littlenose was almost within touching distance of the trees. The log sailed gently along the shore. There an eddy swung the log around and its roots caught in the low-hanging branches of a willow. It stopped, rocking gently. Carefully, Littlenose inched his way along the trunk, and pulled himself into the tree. In a moment he was on dry land – at last!

Littlenose looked about him. Then he pushed his way through the thick bushes to a narrow sandy path. It was patterned with the tracks of animals, but as these seemed to belong to nothing larger than rabbits, he decided he was safe. So he set off along the path in what he hoped was the direction of home.

But it didn't appear to be the direction of anywhere. He could just see patches of sky above him, and the undergrowth on either side seemed endless. The air was hot, and the sand dragged at his feet. Littlenose felt he must sit down for a while, so he settled down against a tree and looked up at the sky.

Suddenly, he sat up with a jerk and blinked.

What had happened? The air was cooler. The shadows were darker. And the sky above his head was no longer blue . . . but pink! He must have fallen asleep. He would have to hurry to be home before dark.

He started to run, but stumbled in the soft, churned sand. As the light faded, Littlenose had to watch carefully where he was going. He ran with head bent, peering anxiously at the ground. And then he had another unpleasant surprise. Something other than rabbits had made prints in this sand. There were tracks of a larger creature. Deep tracks, and the sand was scattered as if the animal had been in a great hurry.

Littlenose stopped and listened. There were soft chirps and whistles from the bushes, but nothing that sounded like a large animal. At least the creature was in front, so he was safe if he didn't catch up with it. He started walking again, watching carefully, hoping the strange trail might turn off into the trees.

But it didn't. Instead, Littlenose saw that the first creature seemed to have been joined by a second. There was a double line of deep, scuffling prints in the sand. Littlenose didn't know what to do. He had no idea what sort of creature he was following – there might even be a whole herd of them! Then a thought struck him. He bent down and looked closely at the ground.

The larger footprints looked like his own.

Then the horrible truth dawned. They *were* his own! He had been walking in circles.

And, if he had been walking in circles with the river always on one side of him, it could mean only one thing. He had not landed on the river bank. He had landed on an island! He must get off – but how? There was only one way. The log – if it were still there. Without wasting another moment, Littlenose pushed through to the water. The floating trunk was still caught by its roots, and Littlenose lay along a branch and broke away most of the tangled twigs before dropping down on to the log. His weight did the rest. With a frightening roll and lurch, the log drifted out into the current.

On and on he drifted. The air was beginning to chill as the sun moved steadily down the western sky. It grew even colder as the log swung around a bend.

Littlenose shivered, and as he did so he noticed that the river banks were closing in, and the current was beginning to flow more swiftly. And the water was choppy, with small waves which made the tree trunk roll. Littlenose clung on hard. The waves became bigger, and he was buffeted and spun one way and the other.

It was getting darker every moment, too, and Littlenose thought, "If only I drift into the bank while I can still see, I might just jump ashore safely," and at that moment the log gave a particularly violent lurch and swung towards the shore. Littlenose watched anxiously as the bank came nearer, but to his dismay he was swept to within a few metres only to drift away again. But it didn't make much difference anyway: the bank was a smooth, rocky cliff, impossible to climb.

Back into the main stream raced the log. Littlenose hung on, lying astride the rough trunk, his eyes tight shut as the waves poured over him. He expected to be swept off at any moment.

Littlenose looked up as the tree jarred on a rock. Some metres away he could see the bank, but once more it was a smooth rock face.

He looked again. It was the same rock face!

He had been round in a complete circle! Already he was being carried out again, and he was moving much faster. In a few moments he was back where he had started, but farther from the shore. Again and again the current carried the log in a circle, but the circle was a little smaller each time. What was happening? Where was the river taking him?

He raised himself to get a better view, and in the last of the light a dreadful sight met his eyes. All of a sudden he *knew* what happened to anything carried down by the river. He was being swept towards the centre of an enormous whirlpool. The water roared as it raced in foaming circles around a dark pit in the centre. As Littlenose watched, a large leafy branch was swept into the middle and vanished, sucked beneath the black water.

Littlenose shuddered. That's what would happen to him if he didn't do something quickly. But what could he do? Jumping off

the log wouldn't help. He had to get to the bank. He was moving so fast that he felt dizzy, and now he could see right down into the dark mouth of the whirlpool. He watched another branch disappear, then almost fell into the water as something cold brushed against his shoulder.

He looked, but couldn't see anything.

Could it be a monster living in the whirlpool? Then it happened again! This time he was able to glimpse something against the night sky. It was the branch of a tree, reaching out over the river, and it *might* just bear his weight.

The log was approaching the branch again, and Littlenose sprang up as he passed under it. But then the log rolled under him. He managed to grab a handful of twigs, and the next moment he was in the water. He only just managed to scramble out as the branch passed overhead again, and he was too late to catch it. But now he stood up carefully, and balanced himself on the rocking log, which was already on the smooth slope of water leading to the centre of the whirlpool. He kept his eyes on the dark, shadowy shape of the branch against the sky, and as it rushed past he reached up with both hands and took a firm grip.

Instantly, he was up to his waist in water as the log shot from under him, and the

branch bent under his weight. Desperately, he dragged himself up hand over hand while the current tore at his legs and almost pulled his arms from his shoulders. At length he reached a fork in the branch and was able to rest for a moment. Below him, in the faint starlight, he caught a last glimpse of his log as it spun furiously on end, like a huge club brandished by a giant hand, before disappearing into the centre of the whirlpool.

Littlenose shivered. He had almost gone the same way. And he wasn't safe yet. He still had to reach solid ground, and he didn't know where he was.

The climb down to the ground was fairly easy, and soon Littlenose was on top of the cliff, with the river roaring far below. He gathered some dry sticks, and took his flints from the secret pocket inside his furs. Rubbing the flints dry, he managed to strike a spark and get a fire started. Then he curled up in the hollow to sleep.

The sound of voices awoke Littlenose, and he opened his eyes. Mum, Dad and Two-Eyes were standing beside him. He was home! Had it all been a dream?

No, the scratches on his arms and the wet furs drying over the fire were quite real.

"How did I get here?" he asked.

"Have your breakfast, and I'll show you," said Dad, and as soon as Littlenose had eaten, Dad took him on to the high hill which lay behind the cave. After a short walk he pointed, and Littlenose saw the charred twigs of his fire. A few more paces, and they were gazing down at the whirlpool far below. It looked even more frightening in daylight.

And Littlenose saw for the first time that the river flowed in a wide loop around his home. His adventurous voyage had ended only a short distance from the cave, on the other side of the hill, where Dad had found him. He felt rather silly about it all, but even so, it was a long time before he next went to play by the river.

Littlenose the Hero

It was a wet afternoon, and Littlenose was bored. He was also in disgrace. Dad wagged a finger at him and exclaimed, "That's the last time you come hunting with me. To think of it . . . In front of all those men . . . I'm surprised that they are still speaking to me. You ought to hang your head in shame."

But Littlenose didn't. He wasn't even listening, particularly. He was used to this sort of thing. "We'll get the 'when I was your age' bit any minute," he thought.

"When I was your age," went on Dad, "I was the sole support of my old mother. I was an expert hunter, and my spear throwing was the talk of the whole tribe."

Actually, Littlenose's was too; but only because when Dad had tried to teach him he had succeeded in hurling a spear through the neighbour's best furs which had been hung out to dry.

All this lecturing by Dad had come about because he really *was* a first-class hunter. What's more, he wanted Littlenose to be one too when he grew up. Now, there were no schools in those days, and a boy had to rely on his parents for everything he needed to learn. Sometimes this was very boring, but sometimes it could be more exciting than any school. Dad had already taken Littlenose on hunting trips, but this last one had been different. Littlenose had been allowed to help instead of just looking on.

Dad continued with his lecture. "There must be *something* you can get right," he said despairingly. "When we let you do the tracking you led us right into a lion's den; and we only got away because the camp fire we asked you to light set the forest ablaze and we managed to escape in the smoke. I just don't know!" And he gazed sadly into the fire.

Poor Littlenose! He really did try hard. He really did want to grow up to be as good a hunter as Dad. Of course, that was part of the trouble. Dad was just too good. Why couldn't *he* make the occasional mistake?

People weren't usually right *all* the time. Except Dad, that is. He had a wonderful daydream in which Dad was surrounded by wild animals, including at least three woolly rhinoceros, and only he, Littlenose, could save him; which he did with great daring and bravery and so became the hero of the tribe. But he knew that in reality, this situation would more likely end with his being chased up a tree or eaten by something.

Littlenose went to bed that night very downcast, and over breakfast the next morning he sat silently and thought and thought. There must be some way he could show Dad that he wasn't as stupid as everyone imagined. He was still thinking as he went out to play with Two-Eyes, and didn't even notice one man call jokingly to his wife, "Watch the washing! Here comes the spear champion!" or another who was trying to light a fire and cried, "Come and help us, Littlenose! You can light bigger fires than any of us!"

Littlenose spent most of the morning sitting under his favourite tree with Two-Eyes, and eventually thought of a plan. He decided that Dad was not going to get into a tight fix and require rescuing just to suit him. If he were to prove himself as a great hunter, then he must catch something . . . all by himself. Then he would show them! What to hunt, and how, was the problem. The Neanderthal folk had several methods, and Littlenose considered all of them. Firstly, small game, birds and rabbits were killed with sticks and stones. But Littlenose's stick and stone throwing was at the best of times unreliable. Secondly, horses and deer were either stalked and speared, or chased and stampeded over a high rock. But, once again, Littlenose's stalking was most likely to cause a stampede, and as for chasing, the animals usually got the wrong idea altogether and chased Littlenose instead!

"However," he thought, "if I'm going to be a great hunter, I want to hunt something really big. Like a rhinoceros."

He had heard his father speak of how some tribes had caught these huge, bad-tempered creatures. First, they dug a large hole in the ground. Then they covered the hole with tree branches and leaves and grass, until no one would ever suspect that the ground wasn't solid, and neither would the rhinoceros. When one came along, the branches broke under its weight, and it fell into the hole.

It was beautifully simple. What happened next, like getting the rhinoceros out of the hole and taking it home, was something that Littlenose didn't even consider.

First thing after lunch he started digging. He had a spade made from a flat bone tied to a stick, and found it much harder work than he had imagined. There were rocks to be moved, and tree roots to be chopped through.

His arms and shoulders ached, but by supper-time he had something to show for all his effort. The hole was at least knee-deep. Carefully, he hid his spade in some bushes and went home.

Mum was appalled when she saw him. "What have you been doing?" she exclaimed, as he trotted into the cave.

"Just playing," said Littlenose. "Is supper ready?"

"There's no supper for you, young man, until you scrub all that dirt off, *and* change your furs. You're absolutely filthy. I just don't know how you do it!"

At bedtime it was the same. Littlenose came home even dirtier.

In the days and weeks that followed, Mum became very worried about Littlenose. He was out of bed every morning as soon as it was light, instead of having to be dragged out. Except for meal times, he was out of the cave all day, instead of having to be chased out every few minutes by Mum while she tried to get on with her housework. Except for his getting so dirty, he was like a new boy!

Meanwhile, the hole was getting bigger. Knee-deep, then waist-deep, then shoulder-deep. Soon, Littlenose couldn't see out as

he dug, but he kept on. A rhinoceros was a very big creature and the trap must be large enough. Littlenose was also worried in case someone should find out what he was doing. He wanted it to be a surprise when he arrived home with his rhinoceros.

At last, the hole was finished. Now came the next part of the work. Littlenose searched the woods round about, and collected all the fallen branches he could see. With Two-Eyes' help, he laid them across the hole in all directions until it was completely

covered. Then he spread dead leaves and grass over the branches, and sprinkled earth over that, until you would never have guessed that a deep pit lay underneath.

All he needed now was a rhinoceros.

Looking at the sun, Littlenose realised that it was getting late. It was long past supper-time. He had better hurry. He gave a last artistic sprinkling of grass to his rhinoceros trap, and ran with Two-Eyes in the direction of home.

Mum was furious when he reached the cave.

"Littlenose," she shrieked, "you get more exasperating every day. Where have you been? Dad's gone to look for you. You'd better run after him and call him back, or he'll be out all night."

Littlenose ran out of the cave to look for Dad. He went along by the river, up on the hill, and into the woods. But there was no sign of him. He decided that Dad must already have gone home, and that he had better do likewise or he would be in trouble.

He had only taken a few steps, however, when he heard a dreadful commotion. It sounded like a very large and very angry animal. He looked quickly for a handy tree to climb, then stopped. The sounds weren't getting nearer. He listened again . . . and his heart leaped!

His trap! It had worked! He had caught something!

Littlenose ran as quickly as he could. The noises coming from the hole when he reached it were bloodcurdling. He dropped on to all fours and crept carefully forward. The shadows in the pit made it difficult to see much, but as his eyes grew accustomed to the dim light, he saw, covered with earth, dead leaves and grass, and roaring with rage as he tried to climb out . . . Dad!

For a dreadful moment there was silence. Then Dad bellowed, "Don't just stand there! Get me out!"

Littlenose looked around. He saw a slender sapling growing by the pit. "Don't

go away, Dad. I'll be back," he said, and dashed away in the direction of home.

Mum was startled when Littlenose rushed into the cave, seized an axe and rushed out again. Back at the trap, he quickly chopped through the stem of the sapling, so that it toppled over with one end in the hole. In a moment Dad had scrambled up and out.

Littlenose had just decided to run when,

to his astonishment, there was a great burst of cheering.

All the men of the tribe were gathered round, and before he could move, he felt himself lifted up on to broad shoulders and carried at the head of a torchlight procession. The men sang as they marched, and at last Littlenose found himself set down in front of the Old Man. He put his hand on Littlenose's head and made a long speech, most of which Littlenose didn't understand. He just stood in a daze in front of everyone. He could see Dad with a very odd expression on his face, and Mum smiling with tears streaming down her cheek as the Old Man concluded his speech with, ". . . and so, to a brave lad who, as befits the son of a great hunter, saved his father from the perils of the dark forest, I present this token."

And he handed Littlenose a boy-sized hunting spear.

Once again, everybody cheered, this time shouting, "Speech! Speech!"

But Littlenose only smiled happily and said, "Thank you."

And so Littlenose became a hero, not that it made any real difference. He was still Littlenose, the naughty boy of the tribe, and even if he *had* rescued Dad from the rhinoceros trap, Dad had a pretty good idea whose fault it was that he had required rescuing in the first place. Also, people soon stopped saying things like A *Hero Wouldn't Do This,* or A *Hero Wouldn't Do That.* Even the spear presented by the Old Man lay forgotten at the back of the cave. In almost no time at all Littlenose and Two-Eyes were playing happily together with no thoughts of brave deeds, but simply having fun. And that is much more important for small boys and mammoths.

100,000 YEARS AGO people wore no clothes. They lived in caves and hunted animals for food. They were called NEANDERTHAL.

50,000 YEARS AGO when Littlenose lived, clothes were made out of fur. But now there were other people. Littlenose called them Straightnoses. Their proper name is HOMO SAPIENS.

5,000 YEARS AGO there were no Neanderthal people left. People wore cloth as well as fur. They built in wood and stone. They grew crops and kept cattle.

1,000 YEARS AGO towns were built, and men began to travel far from home by land and sea to explore the world.

500 YEARS AGO towns became larger, as did the ships in which men travelled. The houses they built were very like those we see today.

100 YEARS AGO people used machines to do a lot of the harder work. They could now travel by steam train. Towns and cities became very big, with factories as well as hous

TODAY we don't hunt for our food, but buy it in shops. We travel by car and aeroplane. Littlenose would not understand any of this. Would YOU like to live as Littlenose did?

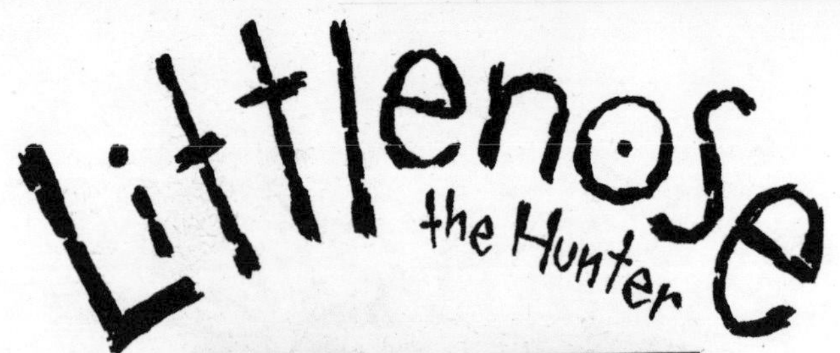

Littlenose is learning to hunt. He has to practise tracking dangerous animals and spear-throwing. Sometimes he's even allowed to join the grown-ups on hunting expeditions.

But being a caveboy is a dangerous business – there is plenty of opportunity to get into dangerous scrapes, and Littlenose is particularly good at that. He just can't stay out of trouble!

ISBN: 1-416-91090-5